SAY THEIR NAMES
SAY THEIR NAMES
SAY THEIR NAMES
SAY THEIR NAMES
SAY THEIR NAMES
SAY THEIR NAMES
SAY THEIR NAMES
SAY THEIR NAMES
SAY THEIR NAMES
SAY THEIR NAMES
SAY THEIR NAMES
SAY THEIR NAMES

written by Caroline Brewer

illustrated by Adrian Brandon

Mama. Daddy.
I want to say their names.
Get out the backseat.
Put a pause on my games.
Color outside the lines,
and loudly proclaim
love for myself

as
I
say
their
names.

I look around at
the broken, the battered.
I hear the cries of
the scorned, the tattered.
I feel the angels weep
because these lives mattered.

And it makes me
want to say their names.

I hear the storm of
Black anger and sound.
I feel heavy hearts
and itchy feet pound.
I see us coming up
from the underground.

And it makes me want to
say their names.

I hear demands for love,
for a cease
to so many of our people
being made deceased.
I see a new day
for justice, for peace.

And
it
makes
me
want
to
say
their
names.

Aiyana Stanley-Jones,
Breonna Taylor,
Charleena Lyles,
Eleanor Bumpurs,
India Kager,
Korryn Gaines,
Michelle Cusseaux,
Sandra Bland.

Ball your fist.
Push up your hand.
We, the people,
must take a stand.
Change gon' come
with our demands.

C'mon and
say their names!

Amadou Diallo,
Eric Garner,
Freddie Gray,
George Floyd,
Jordan Davis,
Michael Brown,
Philando Castile,
Trayvon Martin,
Tamir Rice,
They paid a price.

Ball your fist.
Push up your hand.
We, the people,
must take a stand.
Change gon' come
with our demands.

C'mon
and
say
their
names!

Daddy said
for more than
four hundred years
we've been facing our
worst fears,
we've been drying our
heavy tears,
we've been fighting hard
right here.

C'mon and say their names.

Mama said
we, the people,
darker than blue.
Mama said
we, the people,
know the truth.
Mama said
good people come
in every hue.
So, I ask, we, the people,
"What we gon' do?"

C'mon
and
say
their
names.

I see you, and you see me,
from shoulder to shoulder,
from sea to sea.
Let's breathe in justice.
Let's breathe out peace.
From the North to the South,
from the West to the East.

C'mon and say their names.

Let's perfume the planet.
Let's say their names.
Let rivers of love
wash away this pain.
Love for our oneness,
we loudly proclaim.

C'mon
and
say
their
names.

Speak light.
Say their names.
Speak love.
Say their names.
Speak freedom.
Say their names.
Rise, children! Rise!
Say their names.

Ball your fist.
Push up your hand.
We, the people,
must take a stand.
Change gon' come
with our demands.

C'mon and
say their names.

CAROLINE BREWER

is the Indiana-born daughter of an Alabama-born storyteller. She hopes to one day tell stories as well as her mom. For now, when Caroline writes from her home in Washington, DC, she commits to her words making worlds where peace and harmony reign, where everybody's dancing on a soul-to-soul train.

ADRIAN BRANDON

is a Brooklyn-based artist from Seattle, Washington. He creates work to broaden the narrative around the Black experience in hopes that we can all move forward with greater empathy and understanding.